dopehri

dopehri

PANKAJ KAPUR

Translated from the Hindustani by Rahul Soni

HARPER**PERENNIAL**

An Imprint of HarperCollins *Publishers*

First published in English in India in 2019 by Harper Perennial
An imprint of HarperCollins *Publishers*
A-75, Sector 57, Noida, Uttar Pradesh 201301, India
www.harpercollins.co.in

2 4 6 8 10 9 7 5 3 1

P-ISBN: 978-93-5357-097-2
E-ISBN: 978-93-5357-098-9

Typeset in 11/15.1 Adobe Caslon Pro
Manipal Digital Systems, Manipal

Printed and bound at
Thomson Press (India) Ltd

Dopehri is dedicated to all those people
who forgot themselves in the passing of time,
and age, and relationships...

Foreword

When a fire smoulders, smoke rises up from it. When an intense longing burns deep inside the heart, it evolves into a form that looks like 'Amma Bi'. A stillness, a solitude, like the warmth of a December afternoon.

Dopehri.

Why and how?

Pen touched paper, and Amma Bi came to life. A matter of four days, the play of paper and pen. Despite writing through the nights, it was *Dopehri* – a noontime tale – that was born. Written in the form that I know.

My typist Prem Singh, my children and family were the first victims of *Dopehri*.

When my dear old friend, poet and writer Akshay, heard it, he told my wife Supriya, 'It should be published.' So, many years ago, the first witness to *Dopehri* was the journal *Sakshatkar* that used to be published from Bhopal.

When the then-director of the National School of Drama, Shri Ram Gopal Bajaj, heard it, he said, 'You should read it on stage.' So that's how *Dopehri* became a show for the stage.

When my friend Kamal Tiwari saw and heard it, he organized a show in Chandigarh. Those who heard and saw the show decided that this was an endeavour which should continue.

More than fifty stage shows of *Dopehri* have now taken place all over the world, and the endeavour is still alive and still continues with zeal and enthusiasm. My Supriya's hard work brought it, through Kanishka Gupta, to HarperCollins.

Good, sensible sort of people.

So *Dopehri* has been published and is now in your hands, and ready to submit to your eyes and understanding.

I am thankful to Rahul Soni, who is its editor, who also translated it into English, and also indulged me a little.

If you enjoy it while reading,
if you remember your mother or grandmother,
if it sometimes makes you smile or laugh,
and makes your eyes well up,
and makes you think of your own home –
then I will believe that this attempt has not
been in vain.

dopehri

1

Amma Bi turned on her large bed and fixed her eyes upon the big clock. It was one minute to three. Her sense of time was accurate as always, and she kept staring at the clock until it struck the hour. Her sixty-five-year-old, unspectacled gaze slipped over the walls and stopped at the door, through which she anxiously began to look at the courtyard. It was pouring sunlight outside. She waited to hear some terrifying sound. Her hand reached for the telephone, and she looked at her deceased husband's life-sized portrait a couple of times with reproachful eyes.

She heard a sound, as if someone had leapt in. She gathered all her courage and sat up in bed,

pulled out an old-fashioned blade-tipped staff
that she had hidden away under her quilt, and
began to wait for the one, the same one who came
every day at three and then disappeared. Ghosts
don't come out during the day, so who is this who
won't let me die in peace even in my old age?

The sound of footsteps, the rustling of leaves,
a shadow outside the door. Who is it? And then,
vanished! Drenched in sweat, Amma Bi looked
around for help. Every object in the room was in
its place, curled up from the cold, while outside
the month of December smiled.

Why doesn't that wretched Jumman just stay
here all day? At least there'd be someone to catch
this shadow which stamps out the peace of my
sixty-five years every afternoon and runs off.

Staff in hand, she opened the door. Outside
was the empty courtyard, and the 1936-model
car which no longer ran on the earth but was a
burden upon it and had plants peeping out of its
windows at many places.

The sun was nice and warm, and the cot was
in just the right spot. Bi took a paan out from a
box and began to chew it. She sighed in relief –

now there was nothing to fear. That fellow never came after three. She cast her eyes over the big haveli, and as she chewed on the paan and her eyes began to droop, her gaze fell upon the 1936 car. She closed her eyes.

The car began to move, and sixty-five-year-old Amma Bi was in her wedding attire again, seated in the new Austin as it was entering the haveli. There was the sound of song and music, but there was no one to be seen except for herself. Alone, she looked at the entire house. It was very large, larger than she had hoped. I am the begum, and this is my domain.

Her feet moved faster and she ran about the house issuing commands. She stopped in front of a big mirror. A red wedding dress at this age, and that too on a widow?

She screamed and woke up. The sunlight had faded. The evening was making its bed in the courtyard, and someone was banging on the gate.

The half-eaten paan demanded attention, and her mouth began to move. She glanced once at that damned Austin and opened the main gate.

3

It was him, Jumman, wearing half-pants and a colourful banian. Bi didn't like him one bit, but she also looked forward to the time she spent with him. He was the only one, after all, who saw and heard her in her old age.

Jumman latched the gate, and like a wind-up toy, began to head towards the kitchen.

Bi couldn't walk as fast as him, but still she went after him, cursing. As quick as a djinn, Jumman washed the utensils, chopped the vegetables and put them on to cook, then announced: 'Take them off yourself, I don't have time today. A girl's family is coming to see me.'

'Arey, who will give your their girl?' Despite not meaning to, Amma Bi had declared war. In retaliation, Jumman broke a plate. Bi immediately waved the white flag of surrender and said, 'You halfwit, what girl will want to marry you in those clothes? Come, wear one of Javed's old shirts and a pair of trousers tonight.'

Bi went out of the kitchen. Jumman opened the fridge, gulped down a sweet, wiped his mouth and followed Bi into her room. Bi knew this as she left the kitchen, but she thought: Let that wretched fellow eat, what will I do if he also leaves me?

The big trunk was opened. Jumman made space on the floor. He knew nothing would be accomplished in less than an hour. He was used to this waiting, and he enjoyed it too because he knew he wouldn't be leaving empty-handed. 'Come live here after you get married.' Bi didn't want to lose any chance to lessen her loneliness. 'I'll give you the back room, and your wife won't be alone. You can go to work and come back in the evening. I and your wife will look after each other.'

'I'll think about it,' Jumman said.

Bi frowned at him and wondered what the wretch was made of.

Jumman's expression was as it always was and always would be.

Bi told Jumman many stories connected to the big trunk, and also told him that when Javed returned with his wife and children she would ask him to bring a pair of foreign-made trousers for Jumman and an American nylon sari for his wife.

Jumman dozed off.

A shirt and a pair of trousers flung at him woke him up. He took the clothes and left without saying salaam. Bi kept looking at him as he went towards the main gate. Her eyes grew moist and she dropped the burden of her loneliness on to the bed which, by now, was used to it.

The sound of the azan could be heard in the distance, and as night fell the gate saw that Bi had collapsed on her bed with a thud, as if an arch in this old, lonely haveli had fallen and come to rest against one of its pillars.

2

The sky was strewn with kites, and voices could be heard in the neighbourhood. Deft manoeuvres were being played out, kites were getting cut down.

Jumman was sweeping the courtyard with a broken broom. Angrily, he snapped the broom in two. Its bristles scattered around the courtyard.

When Amma Bi saw bristles along with her cup of chai in the tea tray, she scolded Jumman heartily, but his stony face betrayed no expression. After hearing her out, he said, 'I'd like to settle my accounts.'

It was as if a scorpion had stung Amma Bi.

'Allah! Will you leave a woman to die alone in her old age? Your father and grandfather worked without pay for this house. I have made you a cook, I pay you a salary, I care for you like my own child. I even invited you to live here ... But you cannot escape your lineage! When you die, you wretch, and before they present you in front of Allah Mian, if your father Memon and your grandfather Allahrakha don't thrash you with hard shoes, then my name isn't Amma Bi!'

This seemed to affect Jumman for some reason. Making a face as if he were about to cry, he said, 'Why do you have to drag my father and grandfather into this?'

Amma Bi sensed victory.

'Have you ever considered this? I will die before you, and if I don't tell your father and grandfather about each and every thing you've been up to, then I'm not Amma Bi of Lal Haveli!'

Jumman began to cry loudly.

Amma Bi picked up her cup and took a sip from it, relishing Jumman's tears more than the chai, then said, 'Okay, don't cry. I won't say anything. Now tell me, what's the matter?'

8

Jumman stopped crying immediately.

'The broom's broken. How will I sweep such a big courtyard with a broken broom?'

'Come, I'll give you a new one.'

Amma Bi took her large set of keys and went through a series of corridors and rooms before reaching one from which she extracted a broom. She also picked up an album, before locking the room again.

She sat in the courtyard eating breakfast and watching Jumman do the sweeping. When he was done, she gave him two rupees.

'Buy yourself some sweets.'

Jumman closed his fist around the money and made to leave.

Bi called out.

'Look, Jumman. If you stay with me through the afternoons, I'll increase your salary by fifty rupees.'

Jumman shook his head.

'Even if you give me the haveli, I won't stay here in the afternoons.'

He took two steps, then turned around again.

'Even if you tell my father and grandfather, I won't. Even if they thrash me with hard shoes.'

And like a gust of wind, he disappeared through the gate. Bi folded a paan leaf, ate it, put on her glasses and began flipping through the album in front of her. She quickly went past the photographs of her husband and began to look at the picture of a two-year-old. Her eyes welled up.

'Why are you crying, Granny?' Husain asked.

When she opened her eyes, she found two-year-old Hushu wiping away her tears.

Javed took a sip of chai and answered, 'Son, because we're going back to America, that's why.'

Bi said once more, 'Jaddu, stay back and look after your home, my son. I'm not long for this world.'

'Why don't you come with us?'

'Should I leave my home? How will I face your father in the next life? And your wife wants to stay here anyway…'

Javed looked at Salma, who just smiled.

Salma said, 'It's all right, Ammi. Let him have his way this time. Next year, I promise, we won't go back to America.'

Bi hugged and kissed Hushu, with hope in her heart. She said goodbye at the gate and stared for a long time after the car as it disappeared into the distance.

The big clock struck three.

Suddenly Bi was scared. She leapt up and grabbed the blade-tipped staff, bolted the door and sat down on the ground. The same sound of footsteps, as if someone was climbing down the stairs. She held her amulet in her left hand and began muttering. But her ears were trained towards the outside.

She lifted her head a little. A stone struck the door with a bang. Bi screamed and fell to the ground. She heard the footsteps fading away. Today she had heard the sound of anklets as well.

After the voices were gone, Bi got up and dialled a number.

Saxena Saheb picked up the phone. He was one of her husband's closest friends, and in all of Lucknow Amma Bi trusted no one more than him.

'Bhaijaan, it happened again today. At exactly three o'clock. But today there was also the sound of anklets along with the sound of feet. Someone even threw a stone at me.'

'Are you all right, Bi? Where's Jumman? Okay. I have a couple of patients. I'll come as soon as I'm done with them.'

Bi felt somewhat relieved. She gathered her courage and opened the door. Outside, the sunlight was shining as before. There was a piece of paper wrapped around the stone. It said: *Tonight, at ten.*

3

*T*onight, *at ten.*

Bi read the words and a shiver ran down her spine. 'This means he'll come tonight as well, and God knows what he intends to do this time.'

Saxena Saheb called to say, 'Bhai, my blood pressure's high today so I won't be able to drop by. Anyway, tomorrow's a Sunday, so I'll have lunch with you as usual. Please ask Jumman to stay with you tonight. If he doesn't agree, tell him I said so. And if there's anything else, don't hesitate to phone.'

'Allah, what will happen now?' Amma Bi muttered. She sat frozen for a while. All sorts of thoughts went through her head. 'Perhaps all of this is Jumman's doing, to scare me. Why does he refuse to stay in the afternoons? But Bhaijaan's suggestion makes sense. I'll ask Jumman to stay tonight, and if anyone comes he can at least make some noise. Two are better than one.'

Bi didn't notice how time passed. Soon, it was evening. Jumman still hadn't arrived. What if he doesn't come today? With this thought, Bi stood up, took her bunch of keys, and dressed up to go out contrary to her nature; she latched the main gate, sat in a rickshaw and headed towards Jumman's house.

It is so noisy outside the haveli. Such hustle, such bustle. How the world has changed. And look at what the girls are wearing nowadays! In a little while, she'd forgotten why she had stepped out of her house. The rickshaw-wallah asked, 'Where do you want to go, Bi?'

Bi snapped out of her reverie. 'Arey, where have you brought me? Turn back and go right. It's the third shack. You wait for me. I'll be back in a jiffy.'

The rickshaw-wallah made a face, but waited. At least he was getting a fare back.

With difficulty, Amma Bi made her way past the mud, the pigs and chicken and somehow managed to reach Jumman's abode. There, she found a gaggle of children. 'Oh dear, I wonder what's happened!' was her first thought.

Pushing past the kids, she peeked in through the broken door. And this is what she saw: There were four people sitting on the cots with their backs to the door, one woman and three men. And in front of them, on a tin can, was someone she vaguely recognized. When she put on her glasses, she realized it was Jumman in a shirt and trousers. Was he sitting or standing? It was hard to say. But in Javed's clothes he looked like one of those scarecrows erected in fields that birds merrily shat on.

Amma Bi stepped inside, causing a commotion. 'You?' Jumman said.

His guests also stood up, such was Amma Bi's aura.

She understood that this must be the girl's family. Jumman pushed the tin can forward for her to sit on. She remained standing. She pulled Jumman aside and said, 'So this is why you didn't come to work today. But if you don't finish up right now and come with me, I'll see how this wedding takes place.'

The wretch was even wearing a tie. Bi could barely contain her laughter.

'I'll come, Bi,' Jumman said, docile as a pigeon. 'But they say they want five hundred rupees as mehr. What should I do?'

Bi felt a surge of affection for the orphan. Turning towards the visitors, she said, 'I will give the five hundred rupees. You just say yes to the marriage. Don't let such a good match slip out of your hands.'

Everyone said salaam. The engagement ceremony was fixed for the coming Saturday.

Jumman changed into half-pants and a red banian, took his bicycle and followed after Amma Bi's rickshaw. Bi didn't have a leash in her hand and Jumman didn't have a collar around his neck, but the situation was exactly the same.

As soon as they reached the haveli, Amma Bi turned into a scared cat and Jumman became king. But he didn't behave too regally, afraid that he might die unwed.

Amma Bi talked her heart out to Jumman. There was still a while to go before ten o'clock, and today Jumman, who used to leave like a gust of wind without saying a word, was her captive.

Bi kept talking, a little to keep away the fear and a little to pass the time. She talked about Jumman's wedding, she talked about her own wedding. She drank a few cups of chai. She took sweets out of the fridge and offered them to Jumman herself. She even allowed him to smoke a bidi in front of her.

Jumman could not understand what was going on.

When it struck nine, Bi became silent. She took Jumman to her room. 'Bring me my dinner, and you eat here as well.'

The food was eaten.

The dishes were kept aside.

The door was latched.

Jumman was handed a staff.

And they waited for ten o'clock.

As time passed, the silence in the room grew thicker.

17

It struck Amma Bi that the room was lit but it was dark outside – they could be seen, but couldn't see.

'Switch off the light, Jumman.'

The whole house began to feel frightening.

Five minutes to ten. The sound of footsteps. Bi got up and peeked outside the door. Someone was going through the courtyard to the staircase. There was the sound of anklets on the rooftop.

The two of them looked out from behind the curtain.

Amma Bi said, 'There's someone on the roof.'

Jumman nodded. For the past ten minutes, his jaw had been hanging open in surprise, as if that was where the intruder's first step should be.

Some voices could still be heard. Suddenly, the clock struck ten. In the eerie silence, the sound was nothing less than that of a tank firing. Bi fell back with a scream. Jumman tumbled on to the dishes, which made an even greater ruckus. It sounded as if there was someone else in the room besides the two of them.

A little while later, when Bi switched on the light, she found all the dishes lying scattered on the floor and Jumman, with his eyes closed, licking at the gravy smeared on his lips.

4

Neither Amma Bi nor Jumman could say when they fell asleep that night. But it must have been late, because their eyes only opened at ten in the morning.

The first thing Bi did was go to the terrace with Jumman. Perhaps someone might still be there, or perhaps they might find a clue to the events of the past night.

Up there, the clothes hung out to dry were bathed in dew. The sky was clear and the sun seemed somewhat shrivelled up from the cold. Its rays lacked the fervent desire to gather up the dewdrops into their arms.

The roof was deserted. Kites flew over the neighbouring houses. It was a Sunday, and the kites looked like many colourful patches upon the blue garment of the sky. Bi and Jumman could find no sign of last night's terror.

But Amma Bi had concluded that no one but thieves would come so late on such a cold night.

The phone rang.

It was Javed.

He said they won't be able to visit this year. Salma is pregnant and wants to deliver in the US. They will come six months later and then stay on in Hindustan.

Amma Bi began to cry. 'Who knows if I'll even be alive then. And I'll only get to see Javed's second child six months after it's born – if I'm alive. Hushu was in my lap before anyone else's…' She couldn't stop herself and began to sing the lullaby she used to sing to Hushu, the same lullaby she had once sung to Javed. She brought out some old clothes as a good omen. 'All right, I'll parcel these.'

Jumman came back from the market. Bhaijaan would be coming for lunch today. Amma Bi herself went into the kitchen and began to cook.

21

A fresh tablecloth was laid out upon the dining table. She wore a nice new sari, sat in the rocking chair and began to sing that lullaby once more. Her thoughts rocked like a cradle between the present and the past.

Saxena Saheb was seventy years young, slim of waist, and his moustache and the few hairs remaining on his head were white and fluttering like a peace flag. He had been her husband's friend since their student days and was like a brother to her. The government had retired him twelve years ago from college, but after two extensions, Dr Saxena had retired the government instead. Though he suffered from high blood pressure, he worked twelve hours a day. His wife had died, and his only daughter was married and lived in Bombay. She came to visit him once a year. Saxena Saheb made use of his time and life running a homeopathic clinic.

Like every Sunday, this Sunday too came alive with his arrival, and Amma Bi's loneliness went off and settled down someplace else for a while.

At the dining table, Amma Bi told her bhaijaan everything, complained about Javed, cursed Jumman, and wept her fate.

'Why don't you immerse yourself in some work, Bi? Life and time will both speed past without you noticing.'

'But what work will I do in this old age? And I'm the begum of Lal Haveli, my son sends me money from America. What more do I need?'

'Money can't buy people, Bi.' Saxena Saheb was, to tell the truth, an admirer of old values, and even though he lived in the present, he breathed the air of a time long past. 'Why don't you keep a lodger?'

'Allah forbid, I'll never. People will think Bi has fallen on dire straits, Lal Haveli has become a graveyard, and her son doesn't even ask after his mother. And who's to say that the person who comes to live here won't kill me and take over the haveli? You don't know, Bhaijaan, what the world has become nowadays. For the last ten years, you haven't even glanced beyond your damned white pills and tiny bottles. I thank Allah that he

23

created Sundays, otherwise you'd not even come for your sister's funeral.' With that protest, Bi also staked her claim on him.

Saxena Saheb laughed and said, 'I only spoke for your benefit, Bi, and you turn around and scold me!'

'And that worthless Jumman, you're the one who's spoiled him. The wretch acts so tame on Sundays, as if you've brought him a bone.'

Amma Bi didn't know that every Sunday Saxena Saheb did, in fact, slip Jumman a bone in the form of a ten-rupee note which he kept gnawing on until the next Sunday.

The strange thing was that no one came at three o'clock on Sundays. This made Amma Bi respect her bhaijaan even more, and that leafless branch of seventy-odd years seemed to her no less than some Tarzan.

Food was eaten, cards were played, paan was chewed, chai was sipped in the receding sunlight, and soon it was night. Saxena Saheb left and Jumman went away too. Bi was alone again in the deserted haveli, and fear bound her to her bed.

Once again the same sound of footsteps, once again the same anklets, and once again Amma Bi travelled all the way to the grave and back. She gripped her amulet tight all night and kept repeating verses from the Quran. The clock marched on like a good soldier, and the haveli – upset at the situation, but having no other option – stood in its place. The night and the desolation grinned. And thus, another day passed.

5

When morning came, it took a while before it could reach Lal Haveli's courtyard. It was still dark inside. All the windows and doors were shut. The curtains were drawn. Amma Bi's eyes were open, but a deathly pall hung over her. If her eyes hadn't blinked at the sound of the clock and she hadn't moved at the knocking on the main gate, then perhaps even life itself might have mistaken her for dead.

Jumman came in as usual, but when he saw Bi he stopped. This had never ever happened before in history.

'What's the matter, Bi?' he asked, jerking his neck.

Bi said nothing.

Jumman turned around quickly, set up a table and chair in the courtyard, shot like a bullet to the kitchen, made a cup of chai, and came back and handed it to Bi. He sat down and stared at the courtyard. Sometimes you could see glimmers of humanity in him.

All was silent for a while.

Bi kept drinking her chai and Jumman kept staring at the courtyard.

'Here.' As he took the teacup from Bi, Jumman's glance fell on her hand. There was a bruise. Bi had gripped her amulet so tight, she hadn't even noticed when it wounded her and left its mark.

Haldi was applied.

Amma Bi looked at Jumman with affection. Her eyes welled up. She said in a motherly voice, 'If you stay here with me, I'll be able to live a little longer.'

Jumman snapped up straight like a thin branch that children carelessly let go of after swinging from it.

He turned when he reached the kitchen door, and cried out loudly from there, 'I won't stay here.'

Tired from not having slept all night, Amma Bi dozed off where she sat. When Jumman finished all his chores, he went up to the main gate a couple of times and came back. If anyone saw him, they'd think he had been punished with going to the gate, touching it and returning.

When he was coming back a third time, he was moving so quickly that he slipped and fell down at the steps, near Bi's feet.

Amma Bi opened her eyes and said out of habit, 'The wretch doesn't even break, God knows what he's made of.'

Jumman got up and disappeared out of the gate. Bi heard his cycle bell in the distance a few times, receding further, and then closed her eyes again.

Jumman was ringing the bell loudly, but there was someone in the way on whom it was having no effect.

Jumman clenched his jaw, closed his eyes and rang the bell again with all his might. The pig lying on the road lifted its neck out of the mud on its left and moved it to the mud on its right.

'I don't have time today, but I'll deal with you tomorrow.' Saying this, Jumman lifted the bicycle over his shoulder and walked through the ankle-deep mud to reach his haveli.

He parked the cycle, locked it, washed his hands and face. He took some food from an earthen vessel, ate it, took out a notebook from another vessel, fed grain to the chicken, leapt over the wall and was gone.

Five- to ten-year-old children were reciting multiplication tables while their teacher dozed.

A voice attacked him, 'There you are, Jumman! How come you're late today, my friend? It's time for school to close.'

Master Natthu was his childhood friend. Their friendship had deepened even further when Jumman decided he wanted to study and Natthu took him on as a disciple at five rupees a week.

Master Natthu was a watchman at the old people's home, on night duty. During the day, he mostly dozed off while running the school. The people of the neighbourhood had given him this space for free, because he was doing such noble work. Jumman took care of his expenses towards paans and cigarettes.

This was the reason why Jumman couldn't stay with Amma Bi all day. Especially during the afternoons.

Master Natthu struck a pair of cymbals. On hearing this sweet, musical declaration of break, the children ran off. Master Natthu looked at his watch as he kept the cymbals back. It was four o'clock. He put on a shirt, and decided to oblige his friend. 'There's no time, but I'll still hold an extra class just for you. Okay, now recite the two-times table.'

Jumman put his feet together, straightened his arms against his sides, looked up towards the sky and recited the entire two-times table by heart, without any help.

Master Natthu said, 'You've come first! Now give me a cigarette.'

Jumman pulled a cigarette out of his pocket and handed it over to his guru.

'I'll buy you some chai in the evening. You'll be at home, right?'

Master Natthu left. Jumman leapt over the wall and fell on to his bed. The bed objected a little but then became quiet. The sun couldn't bear the classical music emerging from Jumman's mouth for too long and stealthily slipped behind the wall.

A graveyard could be seen. Jumman was digging a grave. Amma Bi's dead body lay nearby. When Jumman peeked out of the dug-up grave, Amma Bi's dead body smiled, opened its eyes slowly and said in a monotone, 'You're digging my grave. Wretch, I'm going home. Since you've served me for so long, I won't complain to Memon or Allahrakha. But when I tell them that because of my death poor Jumman couldn't get married and their line died out then, you rascal, if your own father and grandfather don't come back as ghosts and sit on that blasted tin can and thrash you, my name isn't Amma Bi of Lal Haveli!'

The spade dropped from Jumman's hand. There was a loud crash and Jumman stood up on his bed. Terrified, he turned slowly towards the tin can. It was shaking. He ran around his tiny courtyard in terror until an innocent little pup raised its head out from under the can.

The pup saw him and he saw the pup. He heard a voice. 'Jumman!'

Jumman looked at the pup again and began to tremble. He held his ears with his hands, closed his eyes, and began to do sit-ups.

'Sorry father, sorry grandfather.'

'Sorry father, sorry grandfather.'

When Master Natthu had had enough of watching this scene, he gave Jumman a tight slap.

Jumman screamed and ran out of the house.

Master Natthu caught him with great difficulty.

Jumman told him everything.

Natthu said arrogantly, 'Don't be afraid. Take me to Amma Bi. I'll solve her problem.'

6

Evening had deepened by the time Natthu and Jumman reached Lal Haveli. The main gate still stood open just like Jumman had left it.

Jumman looked at Natthu. He was chewing a paan. Jumman's face had turned pale. Natthu spat it out. He felt he shouldn't be chewing paan in front of Bi. How was he to know what conclusions Jumman was drawing from the gate being ajar.

Slowly, Jumman pushed it open further and peeked inside.

The courtyard was the way it used to be every evening, and Amma Bi was sitting in the chair the way Jumman had left her. In her hand was the same blade-tipped staff. Frightened, Jumman went and hid behind Natthu. Now Natthu understood what Jumman was thinking. All of Natthu's authority melted and flooded into his mouth. He struggled to swallow it back and deftly manoeuvred himself behind Jumman. And then he began to push him gently forward.

Jumman's mouth opened, his lips moved a couple of times, but no sound came out.

The staff in Amma Bi's hand fell to the floor. Her eyes opened and she saw Jumman, and another strange creature of the same species as him. Why were they running through the house as if it were a racetrack?

'Jumman!'

Jumman and Natthu came back inside from the gate.

Everything was back to normal now.

Natthu told Bi how people in the old people's home lived together. 'Please come once and have a look. Your life will become bright and cheerful.'

Amma Bi had indeed heard about such a place where people of her age lived, and how they were so well taken care of, better even than in their own children's homes.

Bi thought, 'It's not like I'm going to live there forever. It's just a matter of six months, and by then Javed and Salma will also come back.'

She agreed to visit it the next morning.

That night Jumman stayed back.

The next day, Natthu told the superintendent that he would be bringing a big catch. 'The rest is up to you. But I should get a raise if Bi agrees to stay.'

Jumman went ahead of the rickshaw on his bicycle. This time Bi held the leash a little less tight.

Jumman parked his bicycle in front of an old-fashioned building that was painted yellow. Natthu was standing outside. Bi saw the building and thought it looked familiar. She strained her mind a little and remembered. 'Oh, this is Chaddan's father's haveli! It used to be painted white. Jaddu's father and I had come here after our wedding. Choudhury Saheb had invited us for lunch.' Saying this, Amma Bi went through the door as if it were her own house.

Superintendent Shrivastav-ji pushed his glasses up the incline of his nose and welcomed Amma Bi with great warmth.

'Please come!'

Amma Bi thought to herself, 'If you put glasses on a gerbil, you think I won't be able to tell?' Indeed, Bi found it terribly hard to consider just anyone a human being. They needed to have either the regal manner of a nawab, or they had to possess an inner radiance – these two types she could recognize from a distance.

Shrivastav-ji took Bi into his office.

He poured her a cup of chai.

And when he offered her a paan, Bi thought he was all right.

'Over here, we keep our elders with such exemplary love and respect, they'd be hard pressed to find it even in their own homes in today's rapidly changing, cruel world.'

This statement of his touched Bi's heart.

'Come, let me show you your home. And let me introduce you to some of your family members.'

Big, clean rooms, sparkling corridors, a long dining table, a garden to stroll in, dormitories and single rooms.

'Adaab, Badi Bi,' someone called out from the rooftop.

'Arey, Nanhe Mian, how come you're here?'

'I won't come down, my kite is about to tangle. But if you go into the zenana, you can meet my begum.'

Nanhe Mian and Amma Bi's husband used to compete in flying kites.

'Allah bless him, he has four sons, one better than the other, and they were never short of money. How did he end up here?'

Shrivastav-ji took Amma Bi straight to Nanhi Begum.

Nanhi Begum met her with great warmth.

It was revealed that their sons had kicked them out. Their property had been divided up. All of that was fine, but when their eldest daughter-in-law tried to poison them, they had to leave.

'Everyone here is your own, so time passes pleasantly. Nanhe Mian flies his kite, and I chew my paan. It's not as if we did anything different at home.'

Bi didn't think she needed to meet anyone else. She decided that she would stay there. With all the friendly faces, the place had already begun to seem like home.

'I'll wind up my household affairs, arrange for the five thousand rupees and move here in a week, Shrivastav-ji.'

Shrivastav-ji's work was done and it was getting to be lunchtime, so he didn't come to see her out. Bi herself said, 'No need to trouble yourself.'

As she approached the gate, a voice stopped her.

'Bi, here!'

She looked around carefully and found that it was Nanhe Mian waving from behind a tree.

Bi went towards him.

He begged her with folded hands, 'Just stay where you are. At least you'll be alive. What you've seen here is not the reality. Even if you die of hunger in your own home, you'll be more at peace. Please understand, once you come here, you won't be able to live or die. We had no choice. You still have a haveli of your own. Swear on Bade Mian that you won't even take a step in this direction...' Nanhe Mian wasn't able to finish because someone grabbed him and dragged him to the rear of the building.

Bi stepped out of the gate and looked back. Nanhi Begum was watching her from behind the bars of the windows.

Bi sat in the rickshaw. The faces she had seen inside got in with her. Flustered, she told Jumman, 'Take me to Bhaijaan's place.'

7

Once the tiny pills laced with white powder had gone down Bi's throat, it was discovered that Saxena Saheb's living room and clinic were witnessing such an incident for the first time. It also became clear that Bi had crossed over that line of anxiety beyond which one becomes a foreigner and where one loses control of oneself.

Everything was silent, except for the ticktocking alarm clock. Jumman was standing fearfully behind Bi's chair. When Saxena Saheb gave the remaining two patients their medicines and sent them away, he told Jumman to flip over the board outside. Jumman went, turned the board so that it said 'The Doctor Is Out', and when he came back Saxena Saheb gave him such a scolding that the bone the doctor used to toss him, which he had been gnawing at for all these years, suddenly turned into quinine. 'Why did you take Bi there in the first place?'

Saxena Saheb kept shaking a bottle of small white pills in which he'd put two drops of God knows what, and kept scolding Jumman. Amma Bi's eyes were closed and there was a peaceful look on her face. It was hard to say whether it was the effect of the medicine or of the scolding Jumman was being given. This thought did occur to Bi, though: 'I'd like to see which plate this miserable little cricket will break today, and with what face will he ask Bhaijaan to settle his accounts.'

Jumman's gaze was fixed on the bottle of pills Saxena Saheb was shaking, and in fear that one of them may be used like a bullet to shoot him, he couldn't even bring himself to say that Bi herself had asked to go to the old people's home. But he did decide that, should he survive this, he would not spare Natthu.

When chai was served and Saxena Saheb gave him a cup as well, he felt as if Allah Mian had granted him some more years of life.

Amma Bi took a teacup and lifted her gaze towards her bhaijaan fearfully. Saxena Saheb announced his decision. 'You will get a lodger. And tonight you will stay here.'

Saxena Saheb drew up the text for an advertisement. Then he told Jumman, 'Get up now and head straight to Akhtar Mian of Lal Bagh. Give him this note. There's still time before he goes to press. Take this money, and on the way back bring half a seer of jalebi from Raseela's. Go, quick as the wind.'

Jumman's bicycle went flying through the air.

Akhtar Mian looked at the note and smiled. 'All right. The advertisement will be printed in the morning's paper.'

Jumman didn't dare to eat a full jalebi, but he did look around and surreptitiously lick the little drops of syrup that stuck to his finger while lifting the packet, and decided that he would get jalebis from the same shop for his wedding. On the way back, Jumman fantasized about his wedding night. What he was riding was the bicycle, and what he was seeing was this:

Jumman, wearing a golden sherwani, steps into his room. Sharbati, sitting on the red sheet spread upon the bed, curls up shyly. Jumman shuts the door. It has no bolt, so he secures it with a tin can. Fluttering about like a kite without a string, he reaches the bed, not knowing whether he should stand or sit. He pushes forward a pack of jalebis. Mehendi-covered hands pick up one jalebi. Sharbati eats it and kisses Jumman's forehead. When Jumman touches that mark of her love, his hand becomes dirty.

His cycle was standing at a red light near the Kabutarkhana, and a pigeon had left its mark on his forehead. At that moment, Jumman decided he would destroy that nawab – and all his descendants – who'd got this Kabutarkhana built.

Saxena Saheb explained to Amma Bi, 'We'll get a woman who will stay home most of the time – and I'll personally help you choose the lodger.'

It was night. The haveli seemed lonelier than ever. In the past ten years, Amma Bi had never meted out this kind of treatment to Lal Haveli. The main gate was closed, the veranda was deserted, the fog descended upon the courtyard with greater audacity than usual today – and then the same thing happened.

Someone jumped in – the gate saw it – and leapt towards the stairs. On the roof, once again the sound of anklets. In the distance, the sound of a horse cart moving further away.

Two shadows on the roof embraced each other. The girl was crying and the boy was wiping her tears. 'Mother is sending me away to my uncle in Aligarh for a whole month.'

'Sakina, I will die.'

'Don't say such things, Sirju. I'm going, but if I survive, I will meet you here again. Khuda hafiz.'

With the sound of anklets, Sakina leapt over the parapet and disappeared into the darkness of the small town. Sirju knew that there was no one in the haveli today. He sat on the roof for a while, sighed, looked towards Sakina's house, and the words of a song emerged along with his breath:

Hum intezar karenge tera qayamat tak … khuda kare ke qayamat ho aur tu aaye. With heavy steps, Sirju began moving towards his own house.

If only Bi knew that those wandering souls were poor Sirju and Sakina, she would never, ever have agreed to keep a lodger.

8

In the winter morning, when a tonga stopped in front of Lal Haveli, the main gate saw its own Amma Bi alighting from it. Amma Bi touched the gate with such affection that its old bones came alive, and when she pushed it open with both hands it shrieked as if from joy.

The haveli's courtyard, bathed in yellow sunlight, looked more large-hearted than usual, and Bi's chair and paan box lay there like silent witnesses, saying, 'We'll always belong only to you.' It was then that Bi chided herself. What was I doing, thinking of going away and staying somewhere else? How lonely they all have become in one night without me.

'Jumman, make me some chai,' Bi said, as if to tell the chair, 'Yes, it is me and no one else.' She opened the paan box, and seeing the leaves inside still fresh she was struck by the box's loyalty and said to it with great affection, 'I'll stitch you a new glove.' Bi thought that this made her attentive and loyal paan box happy, and she took a paan, put it in her mouth and softly pushed the box away.

She opened her room. She looked at everything as if she had come back home after many years.

She unlocked the room to be rented, which was filled to the brim with objects.

Bi and Jumman didn't see how they could clean it up before three in the afternoon. It just wasn't possible. In the advertisement, Saxena Saheb had asked prospective lodgers to come at three – thinking he'd see who came to scare his beloved sister with so many people around, and also thinking that in the hustle and bustle Bi would forget about the time as well as the one who came every day to scare her.

It was decided that Jumman would bring a couple of people to help in the evening, and it wasn't as if the lodger would move in that very day.

The clock struck three as was its habit, and time came and sat with Amma Bi in the veranda.

There were three chairs there. One for Amma Bi, one for Saxena Saheb, and one for the prospective lodger.

In the courtyard below was a cot and a bench on which six women of various ages sat, awaiting a decision on their fate.

Jumman handed everyone a cup of chai and the interviews began.

It took Amma Bi about an hour to reject all the women. Meeting them left such a bad taste in her mouth that she ended up chewing a whole lot of paans. Saxena Saheb himself was upset that all this effort had been wasted. Jumman sat angrily with his back towards Amma Bi, and began to attack the flies hovering around him as if everything had happened because of them.

In the courtyard were the empty cot and bench, in the veranda were Bi and Saxena Saheb, and on the stairs was Jumman. It was only when Saxena

Saheb asked Jumman to prepare the hookah that Bi realized how angry her bhaijaan was.

'Now I cannot keep just anyone, Bhaijaan, can I? Please don't be angry.' In reply, Saxena Saheb kept pulling on his hookah.

Jumman put the bench back in the veranda, stood the cot up and was about to place it in a corner when there was a knock on the main gate.

The gate was open; a twenty-five or twenty-six year old girl entered, newspaper in hand, and asked from afar, 'Is this Lal Haveli? Did you people advertise for a room to let?'

Saxena Saheb moved the hookah aside and said warmly, 'Yes, yes, please come. Take a seat.'

The girl crossed the courtyard with great nonchalance, got to the veranda and sat on a chair.

She raised her hand in an adaab to Amma Bi and said, 'Could I get a glass of water please, if you don't mind?'

Jumman was glued to the cot. In all his life he had not seen such a bold and beautiful girl.

'Jumman, get her some water,' Amma Bi commanded. There was something about this girl

49

that she liked, but she also thought it necessary to show her that she was Amma Bi, the owner of Lal Haveli. As Jumman passed, she added, 'Bring some chai as well. The lady is looking a little out of sorts. Please sit back and relax. We're all here and it's not as if the room is running away, it is a part of the haveli. Have you read the advertisement properly?'

'Wah, what a wonderful cup of chai!' the girl exclaimed after the first sip. 'Thank you, Bhai. What's your name?'

Jumman had never got such praise – and that too from someone like her. What happened to him is difficult to describe. Let's just say that he was struck dumb from embarrassment, he ran into a pillar, and his banian stretched to accommodate a fifty-two-inch chest. Or should we say: the axe struck so hard that the young tree was martyred in just one blow. His eyes can be described easily enough, though – they were closed.

Amma Bi took control of the situation.

'His name is Jumman. And yours?'

'Sabiha.'

'Will you live alone?'

'No, you'll be home, won't you?'

Bi liked that answer.

'Look,' Sabiha said, 'the conditions outlined in your advertisement, especially the one about staying home in the afternoons and nights, suit me, because from nine to one and then from six to eight I'll do any outside chores, and the rest of the time, my work is such that I'll have to stay in my room.'

Amma Bi liked this arrangement so much that she forgot to ask Sabiha what her work was.

'Will you eat here?'

'If I live here, where else will I eat? Going by the chai, I'm sure the food will also be delicious.'

Jumman died and went to heaven.

Bi looked towards him and said sternly, 'Stand up straight.'

Saxena Saheb said, 'It will be five hundred rupees including food, my child.'

'That's fine. Here's the advance. But I would like to see the room.'

'It's not ready yet, but will be by tomorrow morning.'

'I'd still like to see it, though.'

Sabiha saw the room and couldn't make head or tail of it. She said, 'I'll come in the morning to help, and I'll also set it up according to my needs. None of the junk should remain here. I want it completely empty.'

Amma Bi's attitude changed, 'This looks like junk to you? Bhaijaan, return the advance at once. And lady, you can see yourself out.' Before Jumman or Saxena Saheb could say anything, Bi placed the money in Sabiha's hand and said, 'Khuda hafiz.'

'Who's dying to stay here, Badi Bi?' Sabiha retorted, and handing her five rupees, added, 'This money is for the chai.'

Bi's ego was hurt. 'Do you know that you are talking to Amma Bi of Lal Haveli.'

'And let me remind you, Bi, my name is Sabiha and we Jaunpuriyas don't bow before anyone, not even before Nawab Wajid Ali Shah himself.'

'Allah, you're from Jaunpur?' Amma Bi melted like wax.

'Why? Don't people live there?'

'Arey wait, my child. Come here. You're from my mother's town, the town where I was born.'

Amma Bi embraced Sabiha and began to cry. Sabiha let her.

Seeing Amma Bi cry, at first Sabiha felt awkward, but then her eyes also welled up. She helped Bi sit down, then said, 'Now I have to live with you. I won't even feel homesick.'

Amma Bi looked at her with brimming eyes and said, 'Where were you all these years, my child?'

9

As he returned from night duty, Natthu picked up two glasses of chai as usual from the teashop on the corner, and fighting off the cold somehow, he reached Jumman's courtyard.

There was something under a quilt that moved every now and then. In all these years, Natthu had never been able to figure out in which direction Jumman's face would be on any given day. When he lifted the quilt, his gaze fell upon feet so dirty that they would soil the earth if they stepped on it.

'Get up, my friend! Look, your chai awaits you.'

Jumman woke up, grabbed the glass in his hands, and with eyes closed and still wrapped up in the quilt, he began to sip the chai. This had never happened before.

'What's the matter? Why don't you open your eyes?' Master Natthu was used to hearing a 'good morning'. The guru was upset at his disciple's bad manners.

'Get out of my sight, otherwise I'll thrash you.' It was the first time Jumman had said such a thing to anyone.

Natthu pinched Jumman's nose, and placing the glass of chai on the ground, he tweaked his ear. 'Abey, you'll never be able to get beyond the two-times table, you cabbage-stalk! Is this how you speak to your guru?'

Jumman flung the last bit of chai on Natthu's face. When Natthu's eyes opened after that sip of chai, they found Jumman standing in a corner holding the historic tin can in his hands. Master Natthu felt that if this atom bomb were dropped it would be the end of an era. Forgetting his status as a guru, he said in a friendly manner, 'Are you angry with me?'

Jumman didn't let go of the tin can, and his voice emerged as if from a deep well, 'You disgraced me by taking Bi to that place. If something had happened to her and she went and told my dead father and grandfather, then I would be the one who got thrashed. Is this how you keep a friendship? Go away, from today I'm no longer your disciple and you're no longer my guru.'

Saying this, Jumman threw the tin can on the ground.

But after all, Natthu was the guru. He said, 'I was so embarrassed, I resigned from my job. But anyway, what's a favour in friendship? I'm going away. Who knows where I'll even be able to get a bite to eat now.'

Jumman cursed himself, 'Shame on you for doubting a friend who left his job for you!' How was he to know that Shrivastav-ji had thrashed Natthu and kicked him out – he'd been caught guarding the sweeper woman a bit too closely.

Jumman embraced his friend Natthu, touched the feet of his guru Natthu, and all the walls that were about to spring up between this Krishna-and-Sudama-like pair fell at once.

'Come with me to Bi's house, beg her forgiveness. There's a lot of work there. Today itself I'll get you twenty rupees, and food from Lal Haveli besides.'

When Jumman's bicycle reached Lal Haveli with Natthu, Sabiha was paying a tonga-wallah the fare. Jumman got off the bicycle and shot like a bullet to the courtyard. Bi was waiting in the veranda. Panting, he said, 'She's arrived, Bi.'

'Then why are you standing here? Help her with the luggage.'

'Yes. I've also brought Natthu with me, so that the work gets done quickly.'

It didn't even cross Bi's mind that he had been the one responsible for taking her to the old people's home, for Sabiha had come today from her mother's town.

Natthu and Jumman placed the luggage in the courtyard and stood like soldiers on either side.

Bi embraced Sabiha and called out to Jumman, 'Make some chai, Jumman, then we'll begin work.' As Jumman began to go, Sabiha added, 'Make it like yesterday.'

Jumman kept walking. He didn't even realize when he kicked two suitcases on the way, when Natthu picked them up, and when Bi said, 'Halfwit, at least look where you walk.'

'And why are you standing like a wrung-out cloth left to dry in the sun? Come, that room across is open, bring out everything one by one into the courtyard.'

Natthu emptied the room.

Jumman served everyone chai.

Amma Bi asked Sabiha about her family. And she told Sabiha about herself.

When Bi saw Sabiha go towards the room after drinking chai, she thought: It's actually daughters who are one's own. I wonder why the world doesn't understand this.

It was night by the time the room was set up. When Sabiha picked a few things from out of the old junk to keep in her room, Bi was so happy that she not only gave Jumman and Natthu extra money but also gave them a whole box of week-old sweets. Some clothes had emerged from the room, she gave them away too.

After many years, today there was someone with Bi for dinner.

When she had eaten, Sabiha hesitantly asked for some chai, which made Bi happy. Her husband had been fond of having chai after dinner. Jaddu, however, was nothing like his father.

Natthu and Jumman were eating in the courtyard.

Bi called out, 'When you've eaten, make some chai.'

Natthu elbowed Jumman, 'Make it like yesterday.'

Jumman's food got stuck in his throat. He got up and looked around, hoping no one else had heard Natthu's words.

When he had put his mind at ease, he drank some water, washed his hands and headed towards the kitchen.

As he went past, Natthu stopped him, 'You've got some top-class luck, my friend.'

Jumman gave Natthu a gentle push with his foot and floated into the kitchen.

Sabiha lay reading in bed for a while, then turned out the light. She couldn't sleep for a long time – the feeling of being in a new place was so overwhelming.

Amma Bi, on the other hand, was sleeping peacefully. The big clock made many unsuccessful attempts to wake her. There was someone else apart from Bi in Lal Haveli – at this thought the haveli, which had been deserted until yesterday, felt a surge of happiness after a long, long time.

10

Some days went by like this. Sabiha would leave in the mornings, come back at one o'clock and have lunch with Bi. Then she would lock herself in her room for three to four hours. Despite the whiteness of her hair, Bi seemed to have become younger. No one and nothing came during the nights, or during the afternoons either. Once again, Bi was astounded by her bhaijaan's farsightedness, and life seemed to come alive again.

A few scenes from the days that had passed:

Amma Bi put oil in Sabiha's hair. Sabiha cooked food with her own two hands and fed Bi.

The taste of Jaunpuri food made by a Jaunpuriya was delicious to say the least.

Amma Bi showed Sabiha around every corner of the haveli, and even told her the story of the 1936 Austin. Sabiha took some photographs of Bi. Bi told her stories of Jaddu, Salma and Hushu. Both of them made plans together for Jumman's wedding, and laughed together late into the night thinking how funny he'd look with his bridegroom's sehra.

And this is how morning came to Jumman's home – Jumman kicked away the quilt with both feet, and with eyes still closed, stood up on the cot and began to exercise. While exercising he also kept muttering something which Master Natthu, standing by the wall at a distance, could not understand.

Getting off the cot, Jumman ran in circles around his courtyard. When he sat down in one spot, panting, Natthu spat the bitterness of his datun into Jumman's courtyard. They were at war with each other these days.

Jumman picked up a bucket. There was a bathing area in the corner of his courtyard. Was

Jumman going to bathe in the cold? Natthu's brains froze. These days the halfwit was even wearing trousers instead of half-pants. He'd stopped studying too, which had put a hole in Natthu's pocket and wounded whatever pride he might have had.

Jumman soaped up his face and began to recite the five-times table – absolutely correctly, even while bathing outside in the cold. It all became too much for Natthu to understand. He leapt over the wall, walked over to Jumman, stood in front of him and pushed the bucket of water away.

When Jumman, with his soapy eyes closed, began feeling around for the bucket and couldn't find it, he became flustered. He stopped reciting the table and stood up straight. 'Who is it?' he asked fearfully.

Natthu said, 'First tell me, who taught you the five-times table? It's been over a month since you stopped being my disciple.'

'I won't tell you.'

Enraged, Natthu emptied the whole bucket of cold water over Jumman and leapt back over the wall to hide on the other side.

The cold water had its expected effect on Jumman. He shivered, groaned, jumped up, sat down, and crying bloody murder he began to rub himself all over with his two hands. In order to drive away the cold – and to annoy Master Natthu as well – he began, through chattering teeth, to recite the five-times table once more. No one had ever meted out such treatment to those numbers.

Master Natthu watched from his hiding place.

Jumman put on a shirt and a pair of trousers, even shoes – where did he get them? He put oil in his hair, combed it with a small comb that he kept in his pocket, and lined his eyes with kajal. Now our lover-boy was ready. When Jumman saw himself in the mirror, he put some of the kajal from his finger on his reflection to protect it from the evil eye.

Natthu called out loudly, 'Make it like yesterday!'

Jumman did an about turn where he stood. He looked suddenly deflated, like a thief caught red-handed, and his mouth hung open.

Seeing that the guru was gaining the upper hand, Master Natthu jumped over the wall and stood in front of Jumman again. Jumman kept staring with his mouth open.

Natthu shook him. Jumman looked as if he had returned from some faraway place and was getting ready to head there again, when Natthu changed tactics.

'Arey Jumman, my friend, will you keep secrets from a friend? I was just wondering how you could have learnt the five-times table since you don't come to school these days. See, even Natthu Master's brains get locked away sometimes – I didn't understand that love could teach a man everything about numbers in a single day.'

Jumman hung his head and stared at his shoes.

'I have some polish. Come, I'll put it on your shoes and make them shiny.'

Natthu asked him while polishing his shoes, 'Does she teach you English too?'

Jumman hid his face behind his hands.

Natthu kept on polishing and Jumman's mouth kept moving behind his hands. From A for apple to Z for zebra, he rattled it all out.

Natthu said, 'Don't let Amma Bi find out.'

Jumman turned pale.

'But who will tell her? I'm your friend, and no one else knows.'

The colour returned to Jumman's face.

'Do you have five rupees, my friend? I don't have anything for lunch today.'

Jumman handed over the five rupees. And when he was about to leave on his bicycle, Natthu pulled out a red handkerchief and tied it around Jumman's neck. Jumman touched the kerchief, straightened his neck, sat on the bicycle and pedalled off.

Natthu kept the five-rupee note in his pocket and said aloud, 'Go on. If Bi doesn't slaughter you after seeing that red kerchief, then I swear Natthu the Master will stop teaching.'

As Jumman parked the bicycle in the courtyard, he heard Bi's voice. 'Jumman, lay out the breakfast. Sabiha has to go.'

Amma Bi sat at the breakfast table and Jumman stood near her. Bi had looked at him from every angle by now, and had scolded him in every possible way. Jumman couldn't bear it anymore. Sabiha was quietly eating her breakfast. 'My, my. Look at that red kerchief. The gerbil's had an oil massage! Did no one tell you what you're looking like? Did dogs not chase you on your way here? Arey, you wretch, your face is like pigeon-shit. Won't it get wiped away by that kerchief? Take it off!' There were tears in Jumman's eyes. His hand moved reluctantly towards the kerchief. 'Take it off, or else…'

Before Bi could say anything more, Sabiha finished her breakfast, stood up and said, 'Let it be, Ammi. He's looking so nice.' And with that, she left.

You can imagine what must have happened to Jumman.

～

It was one in the afternoon, and Sabiha hadn't come for lunch. Bi thought some work matters must have held her up. And anyway, Jumman stayed here all day now.

When afternoon became evening, and evening night, and Sabiha still hadn't returned, Bi began to worry. All sorts of thoughts came to her. For the first time she also thought: Who knows what kind of girl Sabiha is, and what kind of work she does? She doesn't even let anyone enter her room.

Bi went up to her room, saw that it was locked, and came back. Jumman too looked crestfallen.

The phone rang. It was a man, saying, 'Sabiha has gone out of town. She'll be back in a couple of days.' Bi asked, 'Who are you?' but he'd hung up by then. Some man phoned for Sabiha. What kind of girl is she?

Bi called up Saxena Saheb. He wasn't in.

Her eyes went to the lock on Sabiha's room again. 'Allah, I never wanted any lodger to live here. Who knows what's in this room. Keep me and my children safe, O God. I don't know what's going to happen!'

In the night, everything seemed even more frightening and wrong to Bi.

For a long time, she paced up and down. She went to the main gate. Outside – and now, even inside – was the same old deathly silence which Bi was no longer used to.

Jumman followed Bi around wherever she went. He was even more eager to know the truth than her.

After Bi's gaze had fallen upon the lock a few more times, her fear of what might be inside grew so strong that she finally asked Jumman to break the lock open.

In the middle of the night there was a loud noise, and the lock gave way. Fearfully, Bi turned on the light. There was no one in the room. Sabiha's bed, a suitcase, and a lot of toys made of cloth, some complete and some half-done. A rabbit, a bear, a small doll, a bridegroom, a tiger – all of them stared innocently at Bi, and Bi kept looking at them in wonder.

11

When the sunlight crossed the courtyard with stealthy footsteps and settled into the veranda, even the casement expressed its helplessness and tossed it softly into Amma Bi's lap. There the sunbeams stretched lazily and touched her face, and Bi opened her eyes as if to say, 'Yes, I understand, you are one more day of life that I have been blessed with.'

Amma Bi had fallen asleep in Sabiha's room last night, and Jumman had found a corner in the veranda.

When she woke up and saw all the toys around her, she felt as if she may have snapped all ties with this earth. But the walls around her and the house were the same, and that unfortunate Jumman too. Recalling everything, she got out of bed flustered and angry, and woke Jumman up. For the first time in her life, she felt sorry for him, thinking – mistakenly – that it was because of her that Jumman had stayed there all night.

Even her experienced eyes had failed to recognize the lover's passion, being a victim of her class's mindset.

Out of habit, Jumman began sweeping the courtyard.

The phone rang.

The bunch of keys fell from Bi's hands, the broom from Jumman's.

Hearing Javed's voice on the line, Bi felt disappointed. In one month, Sabiha had given her what he hadn't been able to in so many years. Bi cried loudly over the phone, and for the first time she complained to her son about her loneliness. When she could no longer speak properly, Javed asked her to put someone else on.

Without thinking, Bi gave the phone to Jumman. He could manage to put the phone to his ear only after the wire had wrapped itself around his face, and he said just this much: 'All right, I'll inform.'

Jumman gave Bi some chai.

On the pretext of getting some sun, Bi lay down on the cot in the courtyard and her gaze fell upon the 1936 Austin once more.

The Austin began moving again. Now, a sixty-five-year-old Amma Bi dressed in black was seated in the car as it entered the haveli. When she reached her chamber after going past the deserted corridors and rooms, she heard sounds as if of people crying. Her gaze moved to the bed. She stared for a while before hearing Javed's voice. 'Abba has left us, Ammi.' She fell down with a thud.

Amma Bi woke up with a scream, only to find that the Austin was in its place and that Jumman was standing beside her. She glanced at him, then looked around. Everything was the same as it had been for years.

There was a knock on the main gate. Jumman leapt towards it and Bi also rose.

Saxena Saheb stepped into the courtyard. Bi sat down on the cot.

Jumman brought him a chair. 'Chhote Mian had called from America. He asked you to phone him,' he said.

'Is everything all right?'

Bi said nothing.

When Saxena Saheb talked to Javed, he found out that Javed was worried about Amma Bi. 'Everything is fine, my son, and I am here as well. Nothing will happen to Bi.'

Saxena Saheb hung up and went back to Bi – who promptly declared that no lodger would live in her house. 'The day that girl returns, I'll throw her out. There's no place for tramps in my home.'

Saxena Saheb tried very hard to explain to Bi that it wasn't such a big deal, but today he seemed to have no influence on her. As he left, he said, 'All right, call me when Sabiha returns. I will come and settle the accounts.'

Bi lay down on her old bed and began to stare at the big clock.

Jumman started putting the washing out to dry on the terrace.

Bi couldn't bear to stay in her room. She came out to the veranda and stood there for a long time, before going and sitting in Sabiha's room.

She looked out from the window.

Jumman was sleeping in the courtyard, snug in the sunlight.

Bi picked up a half-made squirrel and started stuffing it with cotton. All the toys began to smile, as if they'd known all along that this would happen. By the time Bi stitched up the squirrel, it had begun to feel like one of her own. Evening was settling in. Bi left the squirrel on Sabiha's bed. She woke Jumman up, then had chai.

As Jumman was bringing in the dry laundry, he noticed that a tonga had stopped outside the gate. When he saw Sabiha alighting from it, he ran downstairs shouting excitedly, 'Bi! Bi!' Bi heard him and came to the veranda. 'Bi, she's arrived.'

Bi said, 'Open the door. And if she asks about me, tell her I'm sleeping.'

Jumman opened the door. There she was – Sabiha herself. It was as if Jumman had come back to life.

With his customary speed, he picked up her luggage and carried it to her room. As she crossed the courtyard, Sabiha asked, 'Where's Bi?'

'Sleeping. I'll bring you some chai.' Jumman took a few steps and added, 'I'll make it like that day.'

Sabiha smiled.

Jumman was making chai while reciting the multiplication tables when he heard Sabiha's voice.

'Jumman, come here right now.'

Bi opened her eyes and then closed them again, but her ears were straining to hear every word.

Sabiha was standing outside her room, extremely angry.

'Who broke the lock? Who dared to go into my room in my absence?'

All the blood drained out of Jumman. He couldn't tell her. And he couldn't live without telling her either, from fear that the blame would fall on him.

He pointed towards Bi's room.

'Is your tongue paralysed? Why don't you say out loud that it was Ammi? But why did she have to break the lock? I'd left the key under her pillow.'

Bi turned her pillow over. The key stared back at her. Now Bi didn't know what to do. *The things I thought about my own Sabiha! Tauba, tauba, may Allah forgive me!* She touched her ears.

When Bi went and knocked on Sabiha's door, Jumman stood behind the kitchen door, listening.

'Come in, the door's open.'

When she saw Bi, Sabiha got up from among her scattered things. 'Adaab.'

'May you live long.'

'Please sit.'

Amma Bi sat on the bed and looked on as Sabiha arranged her things.

Sometime later she asked, 'Is something bothering you, my child?'

Sabiha burst out, 'I've got such a big order. A friend of mine in Jaunpur had promised she'd help with half of it. But she's done nothing. Those people will come in fifteen days. If the work isn't completed, I'll never get another big order. To say nothing of the humiliation…'

Sabiha put her head in Amma Bi's lap and began to cry. Bi had not felt such a sense of contentment in years.

As Sabiha cried, her gaze fell upon the squirrel she had left half-made. She sat up like a bolt. 'This squirrel was unfinished.'

Bi got a little worried. 'My child, I came into your room. There was nothing to do, so I completed this.'

'You did this?' Sabiha was amazed.

'Yes, I did. But from now on, I won't interfere with your work. And don't you ever leave without telling me either.'

'Ammi, do you know, your hand is so much more skillful than mine.'

'Oh, stop it.'

'No, really. Will you help me?'

'What are you saying, my child? In my old age…'

But in the end, Sabiha managed to convince Bi.

Sabiha was happy because perhaps she'd be able to finish her work. Bi was happy because she was proving useful to her child in some way.

Sabiha presented a box of Jaunpuri imartis to Bi, 'These are for you.'

Bi ate one. An imarti from her mother's town made her young all over again. 'I'm there for you, my child,' she said. 'We Jaunpuriyas won't let Jaunpur down.'

12

Today, after many years, Amma Bi had set an alarm. And when the sound of the alarm spread out through Lal Haveli, it was as if the haveli's walls, its courtyard and veranda, its rooms and corridors all woke up after years of slumber.

Bi woke Jumman first, then Sabiha. 'Wake up, my child, it's morning. The sun will be shining brightly soon. We should get to work immediately or we'll fall behind.'

Sabiha hadn't expected that Bi would actually do something.

As they drank chai, Bi said to Sabiha, 'Why are you stuffing the toys with cotton? It's expensive. Let's get scraps of cloth from the tailor. That will be cheaper. We'll only put in cotton where it's absolutely necessary. I even have some scraps left from when we'd called a tailor for Javed's wedding. Everyone laughed at me then, but see, they will finally come in handy.'

Many locked rooms were opened again, and Jumman hauled out a big sack from one of them, brought it to the veranda and emptied it there.

Sabiha said, 'Ammi, we still won't be able to do it in such little time.'

'Arey, who says we won't be able to do it? Don't lose heart, my child. Just tell me what it is you want to make and how you want to make it.'

Sabiha showed her a bunch of drawings. 'See, we need to make five hundred such pieces – and we have only fourteen days.'

Bi asked Sabiha about the costs, what kind of cloth was to be used, how she wanted the toys made, what material was required for decoration.

When she'd heard and understood everything, she called up Saxena Saheb. 'Bhaijaan, please send the car, it's important. And please come over in the evening, let's have dinner together.'

Bi and Sabiha went to the market in the car. When Bi bargained over the prices and also won most of the arguments, she derived a strange sort of satisfaction. She didn't let Sabiha pay anywhere. 'You can give it to me once you get paid.' Bi bought cloth, buttons, decorative ribbons and a host of other things.

The next stop was at Nawab the tailor's. Bi said to Nawab, 'Come to the haveli tomorrow with your machine, and bring someone with you. There's work to be done.'

Nawab said, 'Bi, there's a lot on my plate right now. I'll finish up in a week and come.'

'If you're not at the haveli in the morning, I will get your shop shut down myself.'

Sabiha had never seen this imperious side of Amma Bi.

Bi had given Jumman four quilts as they'd left the house, to take the cotton out of and card it. 'They're being eaten up by mould inside.'

Jumman wasn't ready for Bi and Sabiha's return. He'd turned white from carding all that cotton. In order to work, he'd donned the same

half-pants and banian as before. When he saw
Bi and Sabiha approaching, he leapt towards his
trousers. Bi chided him, 'Arey, sit down. Stay in
your place.'

Jumman began beating the cotton with a
stick. He sat with his back towards Sabiha, as if
she would no longer be able to see him.

Bi and Sabiha sat on the cot in the courtyard,
working, and Jumman was thrashing the cotton,
when Noor Mohammad entered the haveli with
a loud 'Salaam Bi!'

Jumman's stick stopped, but he didn't turn.

'Who are you, and how have you entered the
haveli without permission?'

'Bi, don't you recognize me? I'd met you at
Janaab Jumman Mian's house.'

Janaab and Mian? Who is this fellow
addressing Jumman with such respect, Bi
wondered. 'Arey, Jumman, is this someone you
know?' she asked. When Jumman didn't answer,
Bi realized that perhaps it was the unfortunate
fellow who was marrying his daughter off to
this gerbil. 'Yes, yes, I recognize you now. You're

Sharbati's father, aren't you? Jumman's father-in-law to be. Tell me, what's the matter?'

Jumman spoke from where he sat, 'Go away. I'll talk to you tomorrow.'

'Let's talk in front of Bi right now,' said Noor Mohammad and sat on the ground. 'Bi, three Saturdays ago the wedding was to be held. It was fixed in your presence with a mehr of five hundred rupees. I've been making rounds of his house every day for a month now, and who knows why, but he's been fobbing me off. Sharbati has shrivelled up from a rose to a thorn in sadness.'

Bi started laughing. She couldn't stop herself from saying, 'Shrivelled up from sadness for him?'

'I thought if not today then tomorrow, but when I heard that our bridegroom to be was romantically inclined elsewhere, I had no choice but to come to you.' Noor Mohammad began to weep.

Bi glanced at Jumman once. Then she looked at the pair of trousers and the red kerchief lying in a corner. Then she looked at Sabiha, who was looking at her. Bi was astounded. She couldn't understand how it had happened, but she realized suddenly that something like this probably had happened to Jumman.

'Jumman, look here.'

Jumman didn't move. He couldn't move.

Bi didn't think it advisable to say too much in front of Noor Mohammad.

'Go on and make the wedding preparations. The nikah will be tomorrow, that's my responsibility.'

The father-in-law salaamed the son-in-law from a distance and left.

Bi got up and went to Jumman, picked up the stick from the cotton and gave him one lash. Jumman fell on to the big pile of cotton. As the cotton flew up in the air, so did Jumman's romantic aspirations. Coughing and spitting, he apologized. Bi gave him money and said, 'Go on. Go home and prepare for the wedding. And at least have a bath, you filthy moron.' Jumman got up to leave. 'And take these trousers and that damned red kerchief!'

'What's the point now,' said Jumman and disappeared out of the door.

Sabiha asked innocently, 'Who has he fallen in love with?'

Bi stared at Sabiha. 'You.'

'Me?' Sabiha nearly fell off the cot.

She put her head in Bi's lap, and both mother and daughter laughed for a long time.

———

Nawab the tailor was working with another man and a sewing machine in the veranda.

Saxena Saheb was sitting nearby in a chair. Bi had called him, saying, 'Please sit at the haveli, we need to go for a bit to attend Jumman's wedding.'

Sabiha and Bi got ready together. When Sabiha wore a sari of Bi's choice and combed Bi's hair, it was as if all that Bi had ever wished for had come true. Showering her with blessings, she asked, 'Why haven't you married yet? When I was your age, I already had a five-year-old Jaddu in my lap...' Sabiha evaded the question.

The scene at Jumman's wedding was something like this:

Some fifty people stood in the middle of an askew tent, raising a ruckus. Master Natthu stood on a tin can reciting a poem. It went –

The head that wears this turban
Belongs to my friend Jumman
Says Natthu Master
May Jumman's head forever
Stand taller than the turban

Accompanied by shouts of 'Wah! Wah!' many four-anna coins were tossed at Natthu. As he stepped off the tin can to collect them, he bumped into Jumman. The groom, too, had bent down, greedy for the coins.

'Abey, it's your wedding.'

When Natthu stood up, he found that someone had made off with the tin can.

Maulvi Saheb said it was time.

Sharbati said yes at once.

When Jumman had to be asked a third time, everyone fell silent.

Natthu pinched him.

An 'Ai!' erupted from Jumman's mouth and the wedding was solemnized.

Amma Bi gave Sharbati some money and said, 'Come with Jumman to the haveli tomorrow, help us with our work. I'll also give you some clothes.'

Sabiha asked on the way back, 'Why did you call Sharbati?'

'She knows how to sew, she can help us. The more hands we have, my child, the sooner we'll be able to finish.'

Amma Bi had been lonely and sad until yesterday, but in the short time she'd got involved in some work, the lonely, melancholic Amma Bi's face had acquired a radiance that, perhaps, only the hardworking possess.

13

The next morning descended rather lazily on Jumman's courtyard.

When Sharbati lifted the quilt intending to see her husband's face, she encountered his feet instead – which have been described before.

As Sharbati lit the brazier, the smoke travelled to wake Jumman up. Like a frog, he stuck his head out of the quilt and then pulled it back in. Instead of a croak, 'Shabbo' came out of his mouth. When she heard his voice, Sharbati turned her left eye to the right and her right eye to the left, and she shot such a sidelong glance at Jumman that he immediately came and sat next to her. 'Don't look at me like that. I'll die,' he said.

Quickly getting ready, the bride and groom got on their bicycle and headed towards Lal Haveli for their honeymoon. When the pig got out of their way, it occurred to Jumman that Sharbati had brought him good luck, for even his neighbours had started showing him respect as soon as she'd moved in.

The transistor that he'd got in dowry was resting on Jumman's shoulder, a song was playing on it, Sharbati's red muslin dupatta was fluttering through the air, and 'O ji' was pedalling away on the bicycle.

Everyone was so busy working that no one realized when Jumman and Sharbati entered the veranda. The main gate which always stayed closed was open today, and everyone had come together and buried the desolation of Lal Haveli God knows where.

Only when Jumman in his clean kurta-pyjama and Sharbati in her red attire said adaab, did Bi lift her gaze.

'Ai hai, I have to hand it to you Sharbati, you've turned my little lamb into a man in just one night!' Instead of Sharbati, it was Jumman who turned red with embarrassment. He went into the kitchen with the transistor and began to make chai, while Sharbati began to help Bi.

Sabiha was keeping a close watch on how everything was being made, so that nothing went wrong. She didn't even spare Amma Bi when she made a mistake.

Many days passed. A big room had been emptied out. All the finished toys lay arranged carefully there.

When the last one was done, Sabiha hugged Bi and said, 'I never saw my mother. She died when I was little. But meeting you ... I've found something that had been missing for years. Work is a separate matter, but let's never allow this relationship to break.'

Bi wiped her daughter's tears. The bears, the tigers, the rabbits, the squirrels and all the other animals witnessed them. But constrained by their circumstances, they couldn't say anything. They just sat still and made their presence felt.

The general manager of Toys Private Limited himself had come down to inspect the goods. Despite being a businessman, he couldn't help but remark upon how much better the toys were this time, compared to the last. 'I'll send a truck. You can put them in polythene bags and send them to the godown. The packing will be done there.' As he went, he handed over a cheque and also placed a new order.

The truck came and was being loaded. When the time came to say goodbye to the toys, Amma Bi's eyes welled up. Until yesterday they were mine, today they'll belong to the world. But then, these are mere toys. Even people leave you and go away … Bi thought of Jaddu.

Sabiha reminded her that a new order had come – no one could deny them the joy of creation.

At dinner that night, Saxena Saheb congratulated Bi and Sabiha warmly and asked, 'Does nobody come these days, Bi, to trouble you in the afternoons or nights?'

Amma Bi had forgotten about it completely. 'It's true, Bhaijaan. Since Sabiha came, that wretch hasn't dared to venture here.'

'Bi, it was your own loneliness that was scaring you.'

Bi refused to believe such a thing.

'Okay, let it be. Now tell me this – do you trust me?' Saxena Saheb asked.

Bi said, 'In all of Lucknow, I trust no one more.'

'More than me?' Sabiha asked.

'I trust you even more than myself, my child.'

'More than me?' Saxena Saheb asked.

'Go away you two, trying to confuse me!' Bi said like a child, and all three of them burst out laughing, and stayed up until late at night enjoying each other's company.

Jumman had fallen asleep, exhausted.

Sharbati served them all chai after dinner and asked, 'Can we go?'

Saxena Saheb said, 'Ask Bi.'

'I was asking her only,' Sharbati said, looking towards Saxena Saheb.

Sabiha looked at Sharbati closely for the first time. She was good looking, except one eye looked here and the other eye looked there.

'Go. And you can come late tomorrow,' Bi said.

When Sharbati had gone, Bi smiled and said, 'That is the sort of sideways glance one needs to see Jumman straight … The halfwit himself flutters and sways as he walks.'

After finishing her chai, Sabiha asked Bi a question that no one had asked her since her husband had died.

'Ammi, what's your name?'

'Which one should I tell you? The one from my mother's home or the one from my husband's? Before my wedding, I was Tahmina. My mother used to call me Tummo.' Bi sighed. 'After marriage, I became Mumtaz – my husband didn't consider himself any less than Emperor Shahjahan, after all.' Amma Bi blushed as she said this.

Saying, 'I'll be right back,' Sabiha went to her room.

She wrote a cheque in the name of Mumtaz Siddiqui, came back and handed it to Bi.

Bi looked at the cheque and asked, 'What's this?'

'Compensation for all the work you did.'

'Are you mad? I'm not going to take money from you.'

Saxena Saheb said, 'This is money you have earned. It's not charity.'

'My earnings? Oh, let it be. I can't take money from my daughter. How will I show my face to Allah Mian? I have no intention of going to hell.'

It was two o'clock at night by the time Sabiha and Saxena Saheb could convince Bi that this was her right, earned fair and square. That it was something on which no one else had a claim. And if anyone else used it, they would certainly go straight to hell.

'My Sabiha will go to hell because of me? O God, no!' Bi finally accepted the cheque.

When she lay down in bed, she couldn't sleep. Her gaze went to her husband's life-sized portrait. She kept looking at it for a while, then from under her pillow she pulled out the cheque in her name. Mumtaz Siddiqui. She read that name, which had become lost in the passage of years and among relationships. She read it again, Mumtaz Siddiqui. Then she raised her head with pride and showed the cheque to the portrait. Her eyes became moist, but she couldn't say anything.

She got up from her bed and went out of the room.

She climbed up to the terrace.

In spite of the freezing cold, her face was glowing.

She saw that the moon, all of it, was awake.

Seeing Amma Bi, it was as if the moon stopped.

It smiled, then asked, 'Tell me, Bi, what is it you want to say?'

Bi kept looking at the dark, silent, sleeping city.

The moon asked again, lovingly, 'Tell me, Amma Bi, what is it you want to say?'

Sixty-five years of suppressed emotions exploded, and she cried out, 'Not Amma Bi, brother, my name is Mumtaz Siddiqui, and this is my own hard-earned money – you can tell him!'

About the Author

Pankaj Kapur (born 1954) is an acclaimed Indian theatre, television and film actor and director. He has won numerous awards for his work, including three National Film Awards and one Filmfare Award. *Dopehri* is his first novel.